THE SNOW QUEEN

KATE GREENAWAY'S ORIGINAL DRAWINGS *for*

The Snow Queen

by HANS CHRISTIAN ANDERSEN

Translated by Charles Boner

Afterword by Michael Patrick Hearn

SCHOCKEN BOOKS / New York

First published by Schocken Books 1981 / First edition

Illustrations and Afterword copyright © 1981 by Michael Patrick Hearn

The text of this edition is taken from *The Shoes of Fortune, and Other Tales,*
translated by Charles Boner, 1846.

The suite of twelve pencil drawings by Kate Greenaway were studies for an
unpublished edition of *The Snow Queen.* Permission to reproduce these designs
has been granted by Mr. Francis Carpenter, on behalf of the Kate Greenaway Estate.

Library of Congress Cataloging in Publication Data

Andersen, H. C. (Hans Christian), 1805–1875.
Kate Greenaway's original drawings for the Snow Queen.

Translation of Sneedronningen.
Summary / This edition of Andersen's fairy tale features first-time
reproductions of pencil sketches Kate Greenaway prepared especially for the
Snow Queen and an afterword about the artist's life and work.
[1. Fairy tales. 2. Greenaway, Kate, 1846–1901]
I. Greenaway, Kate, 1846–1901, ill. II. Title.
PZ8.A542Sn 1981   [Fic]   81–40406

Manufactured in the United States of America
Designed by Jane Byers Bierhorst
ISBN 0-8052-3776-3

for Jane Yolen
M.P.H.

THE SNOW QUEEN

First Story

WHICH TREATS OF A MIRROR AND OF THE SPLINTERS

Now, then, let us begin. When we are at the end of the story, we shall know more than we know now: but to begin.

Once upon a time there was a wicked Sprite, indeed he was the most mischievous of all sprites. One day he was in a very good humor, for he had made a mirror with the power of causing all that was good and beautiful when it was reflected therein to look poor and mean; but that which was good for nothing and looked ugly, was shown magnified and increased in ugliness. In this mirror the most beautiful landscapes looked like boiled spinach, and the best persons were turned into frights, or appeared to stand on their heads; their faces were so distorted that they were not to be recognized; and if anyone had a mole, you might be sure that it would be magnified and spread over both nose and mouth. "That's glorious fun!" said the Sprite. If a good thought passed through a man's mind, then a grin was seen in the mirror, and the Sprite laughed heartily at his clever discovery. All the little sprites who went to his school—for he kept a sprite school—told each other that a miracle had happened; and that now only, as they thought, it would be possible to see how the world really looked. They ran about with the mirror; and at last there was not a land or a person who was not represented distorted in the mirror. So then they thought they would fly up to the sky, and have a joke there. The higher they flew with the mirror, the more terribly it grinned: they could hardly hold it fast. Higher and higher still they flew, nearer and nearer to the stars, when suddenly the mirror shook so terribly with grinning, that it flew out of their hands and fell to the earth, where it was dashed in a hundred million and more pieces. And now it worked much more evil than before; for some of these pieces were hardly so large as a grain of sand, and they flew about in the wide world, and when they got into people's eyes, there they stayed; and then people saw everything perverted, or only had an eye for that which was evil. This happened because the very smallest bit had the same power which the whole mirror had possessed. Some persons even got a splinter in their heart, and then it made one shudder, for their heart became like a lump of ice. Some of the broken pieces were so large that they were used for windowpanes, through which one could not see one's friends. Other pieces were put in spectacles; and

that was a sad affair when people put on their glasses to see well and

rightly. Then the wicked Sprite laughed till he almost choked, for all this tickled his fancy. The fine splinters still flew about in the air : and now we shall hear what happened next.

Second Story

A LITTLE BOY AND A LITTLE GIRL

In a large town, where there are so many houses, and so many people, that there is no room left for everybody to have a little garden ; and where, on this account, most persons are obliged to content themselves with flowers in pots ; there lived two little children, who had a garden somewhat larger than a flowerpot. They were not brother and sister ; but they cared for each other as much as if they were. Their parents lived exactly opposite. They inhabited two garrets ; and where the roof of the one house joined that of the other, and the gutter ran along the extreme end of it, there was to each house a small window : one needed only to step over the gutter to get from one window to the other.

The children's parents had large wooden boxes there, in which vegetables for the kitchen were planted, and little rose trees besides : there was a rose in each box, and they grew splendidly. They now thought of placing the boxes across the gutter, so that they nearly reached from one window to the other, and looked just like two walls of flowers. The tendrils of the peas hung down over the boxes ; and the rose trees shot up long branches, twined round the windows, and then bent toward each other : it was almost like a triumphal arch of foliage and flowers. The boxes were very high, and the children knew that they must not creep over them ; so they often obtained

· 7 ·

permission to get out of the windows to each other, and to sit on their little stools among the roses, where they could play delightfully. In winter there was an end of this pleasure. The windows were often frozen over; but then they heated copper farthings on the stove, and laid the hot farthing on the windowpane, and then they had a capital peephole, quite nicely rounded; and out of each peeped a gentle friendly eye—it was the little boy and the little girl who were looking out. His name was Kay, hers was Gerda. In summer, with one jump, they could get to each other; but in winter they were obliged first to go down the long stairs, and then up the long stairs again: and out of doors there was quite a snowstorm.

"It is the white bees that are swarming," said Kay's old grandmother.

"Do the white bees choose a queen?" asked the little boy; for he knew that the honeybees always have one.

"Yes," said the grandmother, "she flies where the swarm hangs in the thickest clusters. She is the largest of all; and she can never remain quietly on the earth, but goes up again into the black clouds. Many a winter's night she flies through the streets of the town, and peeps in at the windows; and they then freeze in so wondrous a manner that they look like flowers."

"Yes, I have seen it," said both the children; and so they knew that it was true.

"Can the Snow Queen come in?" said the little girl.

"Only let her come in!" said the little boy; "then I'd put her on the stove, and she'd melt."

And then his grandmother patted his head, and told him other stories.

In the evening, when little Kay was at home, and half undressed, he climbed upon the chair by the window, and peeped out of the little hole. A few snowflakes were falling, and one, the largest of all, remained lying on the edge of a flowerpot. The flake of snow grew larger and larger; and at last it was like a young lady, dressed in the finest white gauze, made of a million little flakes, like stars. She was so beautiful and delicate, but she was of ice, of dazzling, sparkling ice; yet she lived; her eyes gazed fixedly,

like two stars; but there was neither quiet nor repose in them. She nodded toward the window, and beckoned with her hand. The little boy was frightened, and jumped down from the chair; it seemed to him as if, at the same moment, a large bird flew past the window.

The next day it was a sharp frost—and then the spring came; the sun shone, the green leaves appeared, the swallows built their nests, the windows were opened, and the little children again sat in their pretty garden, high up on the leads at top of the house.

That summer the roses flowered in unwonted beauty. The little girl had learned a hymn, in which there was something about roses; and then she thought of her own flowers; and she sang the verse to the little boy, who then sang it with her:

> The rose in the valley is blooming so sweet,
> And angels descend there the children to greet.

And the children held each other by the hand, kissed the roses, looked up at the clear sunshine, and spoke as though they really saw angels there. What lovely summer days those were! How delightful to be out in the air, near the fresh rosebushes, that seem as if they would never finish blossoming!

Kay and Gerda looked at the picture book full of beasts and of birds; and it was then—the clock in the church tower was just striking five—that Kay said, "Oh! I feel such a sharp pain in my heart; and now something has got into my eye!"

The little girl put her arms round his neck. He winked his eyes—now, there was nothing to be seen.

"I think it is out now," said he; but it was not. It was just one of those pieces of glass from the magic mirror that had got into his eye; and poor Kay had got another piece right in his heart. It will soon become like ice. It did not hurt any longer, but there it was.

"What are you crying for?" asked he. "You look so ugly! There's nothing the matter with me. Ah," said he at once, "that rose is cankered! and, look, this one is quite crooked! after all, these roses are very ugly! they are just like the box they are planted in!" And then he gave the box a good kick with his foot, and pulled both the roses up.

"What are you doing?" cried the little girl; and as he perceived her fright, he pulled up another rose, got in at the window, and hastened off from dear little Gerda.

Afterward, when she brought her picture book, he asked, "What horrid beasts had she there?" And if his grandmother told them stories, he always interrupted her; besides, if he could manage it, he would get behind her, put on her spectacles, and imitate her way of speaking: he copied all her ways, and then everybody laughed at him. He was soon able to imitate the gait and manner of everyone in the street. Everything that was peculiar and displeasing in them—that Kay knew how to imitate; and at such times all the people said. "The boy is certainly very clever!" But it was the glass

he had got in his eye; the glass that was sticking in his heart, which made him tease even little Gerda, whose whole soul was devoted to him.

His games now were quite different to what they had formerly been, they were so very knowing. One winter's day, when the flakes of snow were flying about, he spread the skirts of his blue coat, and caught the snow as it fell.

"Look through this glass, Gerda," said he. And every flake seemed larger, and appeared like a magnificent flower, or a beautiful star: it was splendid to look at!

"Look, how clever!" said Kay. "That's much more interesting than real flowers! They are as exact as possible; there is not a fault in them; if they did not melt!"

It was not long after this that Kay came one day with large gloves on and his little sledge at his back and bawled right into Gerda's ears, "I have permission to go out into the square where the others are playing"; and off he was in a moment.

There, in the marketplace, some of the boldest of the boys used to tie their sledges to the carts as they passed by, and so they were pulled along and got a good ride. It was so capital! Just as they were in the very height of their amusement, a large sledge passed by: it was painted quite white, and there was someone in it wrapped up in a rough white mantle of fur, with a rough white fur cap on his head. The sledge drove round the square twice, and Kay tied on his as quickly as he could, and off he drove with it. On they went, quicker and quicker into the next street; and the person who drove turned round to Kay, and nodded to him in a friendly manner, just as if they knew each other. Every time he was going to untie his sledge the person nodded to him, and then Kay sat quiet; and so on they went till they came outside the gates of the town. Then the snow began to fall so thickly, that the little boy could not see an arm's length before him, but still on he went; when suddenly he let go the string he held in his hand in order to get loose from the sledge, but it was of no use; still the little vehicle rushed on with the quickness of the wind. He then cried as loud as he could, but no one heard him; the snow drifted and the sledge flew on, and sometimes it gave a jerk as though they were driving over hedges and ditches. He was quite frightened, and he tried to repeat the Lord's Prayer; but all he could do, he was only able to remember the multiplication table.

The snowflakes grew larger and larger, till at last they looked just like great white fowl. Suddenly they flew on one side; the large sledge stopped, and the person who drove rose up. It was a lady; her cloak and cap were of snow. She was tall and of slender figure, and of a dazzling whiteness. It was the Snow Queen.

"We have traveled fast," said she; "but it is freezingly cold. Come under my bearskin." And she put him in the sledge beside her, wrapped the fur round him, and he felt as though he were sinking in a snow wreath.

"Are you still cold?" asked she; and then she kissed his forehead. Ah! it was colder than ice; it penetrated to his very heart, which was already almost a frozen lump; it seemed to him as if he were about to die—but a moment more and it was quite congenial to him, and he did not remark the cold that was around him.

"My sledge! Do not forget my sledge!" It was the first thing he thought of. It was there tied to one of the white chickens, who flew along with it on its back behind the large sledge. The Snow Queen kissed Kay once more, and then he forgot little Gerda, grandmother, and all whom he had left at his home.

"Now you will have no more kisses," said she, "or else I should kiss you to death!"

Kay looked at her. She was very beautiful; a more clever or a more lovely countenance he could not fancy to himself; and she no longer appeared of ice as before, when she sat outside the window, and beckoned to him; in his eyes she was perfect, he did not fear her at all, and told her that he could calculate in his head, and with fractions even; that he knew the number of square miles there were in the different countries, and how many inhabit-ants they contained; and she smiled while he spoke. It then seemed to him

as if what he knew was not enough, and he looked upward in the large huge empty space above him, and on she flew with him; flew high over the black clouds, while the storm moaned and whistled as though it were singing some old tune. On they flew over woods and lakes, over seas and many lands; and beneath them the chilling storm rushed fast, the wolves howled, the snow crackled; above them flew large screaming crows, but higher up appeared the moon quite large and bright; and it was on it that Kay gazed during the long long winter's night; while by day he slept at the feet of the Snow Queen.

Third Story

OF THE FLOWER GARDEN AT THE OLD WOMAN'S WHO UNDERSTOOD WITCHCRAFT

But what became of little Gerda when Kay did not return? Where could he be? Nobody knew; nobody could give any intelligence. All the boys knew was, that they had seen him tie his sledge to another large and splendid one, which drove down the street and out of the town. Nobody knew where he was; many sad tears were shed, and little Gerda wept long and bitterly: at last she said he must be dead; that he had been drowned in the river which flowed close to the town. Oh! those were very long and dismal winter evenings.

At last spring came with its warm sunshine.

"Kay is dead and gone!" said little Gerda.

"That I don't believe," said the Sunshine.

"Kay is dead and gone!" said she to the Swallows.

"That I don't believe," said they; and at last little Gerda did not think so any longer either.

"I'll put on my red shoes," said she, one morning; "Kay has never seen them, and then I'll go down to the river and ask there."

It was quite early: she kissed her old grandmother, who was still asleep, put on her red shoes, and went alone to the river.

"Is it true that you have taken my little playfellow? I will make you a present of my red shoes, if you will give him back to me."

And, as it seemed to her, the blue waves nodded in a strange manner; then she took off her red shoes, the most precious things she possessed, and threw them both into the river. But they fell close to the bank, and the little waves bore them immediately to land; it was as if the stream would not take what was dearest to her; for in reality it had not got little Kay: but Gerda thought that she had not thrown the shoes far out enough, so she clambered into a boat which lay among the rushes, went to the farthest end, and threw out the shoes. But the boat was not fastened, and the motion which she occasioned, made it drift from the shore. She observed this, and hastened to get back; but before she could do so, the boat was more than a yard from the land, and was gliding quickly onward.

Little Gerda was very frightened, and began to cry; but no one heard her except the sparrows, and they could not carry her to land; but they flew along the bank, and sang as if to comfort her, "Here we are! here we are!" The boat drifted with the stream, little Gerda sat quite still without shoes, for they were swimming behind the boat, but could not reach it, because it went much faster than they did.

The banks on both sides were beautiful; lovely flowers, venerable trees, and slopes with sheep and cows, but not a human being was to be seen.

"Perhaps the river will carry me to little Kay," said she; and then she grew less sad. She rose, and looked for many hours at the beautiful green banks. Presently she sailed by a large cherry orchard, where was a little

cottage with curious red and blue windows; it was thatched, and before it two wooden soldiers stood sentry, and presented arms when anyone went past.

Gerda called to them, for she thought they were alive; but they, of course, did not answer. She came close to them, for the stream drifted the boat quite near the land.

Gerda called still louder, and an old woman then came out of the cottage, leaning upon a crooked stick. She had a large broad-brimmed hat on, painted with the most splendid flowers.

"Poor little child!" said the old woman, "how did you get upon the large rapid river, to be driven about so in the wide world!" And then the old woman went into the water, caught hold of the boat with her crooked stick, drew it to the bank, and lifted little Gerda out.

And Gerda was so glad to be on dry land again; but she was rather afraid of the strange old woman.

"But come and tell me who you are, and how you came here," said she.

And Gerda told her all; and the old woman shook her head and said, "A-hem! a-hem!" and when Gerda had told her everything, and asked her if she had not seen little Kay, the woman answered that he had not passed there, but he no doubt would come; and she told her not to be cast down, but taste her cherries, and look at her flowers, which were finer than any in a picture book, each of which could tell a whole story. She then took Gerda by the hand, led her into the little cottage, and locked the door.

The windows were very high up; the glass was red, blue, and green, and the sunlight shone through quite wondrously in all sorts of colors. On the table stood the most exquisite cherries, and Gerda ate as many as she chose, for she had permission to do so. While she was eating, the old woman combed her hair with a golden comb, and her hair curled and shone with a lovely golden color around that sweet little face, which was so round, and so like a rose.

"I have often longed for such a dear little girl," said the old woman.

· 21 ·

"Now you shall see how well we agree together"; and while she combed little Gerda's hair, the child forgot her foster-brother Kay more and more, for the old woman understood magic; but she was no evil being, she only practiced witchcraft a little for her own private amusement, and now she wanted very much to keep little Gerda. She therefore went out into the garden, stretched out her crooked stick toward the rosebushes, which, beautifully as they were blowing, all sank into the earth, and no one could tell where they had stood. The old woman feared that if Gerda should see the roses, she would then think of her own, would remember little Kay, and run away from her.

She now led Gerda into the flower garden. Oh, what odor and what loveliness was there! Every flower that one could think of, and of every season, stood there in fullest bloom : no picture book could be gayer or more beautiful. Gerda jumped for joy, and played till the sun set behind the tall cherry tree; she then had a pretty bed, with a red silken coverlet filled with blue violets. She fell asleep, and had as pleasant dreams as ever a queen on her wedding day.

The next morning she went to play with the flowers in the warm sunshine, and thus passed away a day. Gerda knew every flower; and, numerous as they were, it still seemed to Gerda that one was wanting, though she did not know which. One day while she was looking at the hat of the old woman painted with flowers, the most beautiful of them all seemed to her to be a rose. The old woman had forgotten to take it from her hat when she made the others vanish in the earth. But so it is when one's thoughts are not collected. "What!" said Gerda; "are there no roses here?" and she ran about among the flower beds, and looked, and looked, but there was not one to be found. She then sat down and wept; but her hot tears fell just where a rosebush had sunk; and when her warm tears watered the ground, the tree shot up suddenly as fresh and blooming as when it had been swallowed up. Gerda kissed the roses, thought of her own dear roses at home, and with

them of little Kay.

"Oh, how long I have stayed!" said the little girl. "I intended to look for Kay! Don't you know where he is?" asked she of the Roses. "Do you think he is dead and gone?"

"Dead he certainly is not," said the Roses. "We have been in the earth where all the dead are, but Kay was not there."

"Many thanks!" said the little Gerda; and she went to the other flowers, looked into their cups, and asked, "Don't you know where little Kay is?"

But every flower stood in the sunshine, and dreamed its own fairy tale or its own story; and they all told her very many things, but not one knew anything of Kay.

Well, what did the Tiger Lily say?

"Hearest thou not the drum? Bum! bum! those are the only two tones. Always bum! bum! Hark to the plaintive song of the old woman! to the call of the priests! The Hindu woman in her long robe stands upon the funeral pile: the flames rise around her and her dead husband, but the Hindu woman thinks on the living one in the surrounding circle; on him whose eyes burn hotter than the flames—on him, the fire of whose eyes pierces her heart more than the flames which soon will burn her body to ashes. Can the heart's flame die in the flame of the funeral pile?"

"I don't understand that at all," said little Gerda.

"That is my story," said the Lily.

What did the Convolvulus say?

"Projecting over a narrow mountain path, there hangs an old feudal castle. Thick evergreens grow on the dilapidated walls and around the altar, where a lovely maiden is standing: she bends over the railing and looks out upon the rose. No fresher rose hangs on the branches than she; no apple blossom carried away by the wind is more buoyant! How her splendid silken robe is rustling!

"'Is he not yet come?'"

"Is it Kay that you mean?" asked little Gerda.

"I am speaking about my story—about my dream," answered the Convolvulus.

What did the Snowdrops say?

"Between the trees a long board is hanging—it is a swing. Two little girls are sitting in it, and swing themselves backward and forward: their frocks are as white as snow, and long green silk ribbons flutter from their bonnets. Their brother, who is older than they are, stands up in the swing; he twines his arms round the cords to hold himself fast, for in one hand he has a little cup, and in the other a clay pipe. He is blowing soap bubbles. The swing moves, and the bubbles float in charming changing colors: the last is still hanging to the end of the pipe, and rocks in the breeze. The swing moves. The little black dog, as light as a soap bubble, jumps up on his hind legs to try to get into the swing. It moves, the dog falls down, barks, and is angry. They tease him; the bubble bursts! A swing, a bursting bubble—such is my song!"

"What you relate may be very pretty, but you tell it in so melancholy a manner, and do not mention Kay."

What do the Hyacinths say?

"There were once upon a time three sisters, quite transparent and very beautiful. The robe of the one was red, that of the second blue, and that of the third white. They danced hand in hand beside the calm lake in the clear moonshine. They were not elfin maidens, but mortal children. A sweet fragrance was smelled, and the maidens vanished in the wood; the fragrance grew stronger: three coffins, and in them three lovely maidens, glided out of the forest and across the lake: the shining glowworms flew around like little floating lights. Do the dancing maidens sleep, or are they dead? The odor of the flowers says they are corpses; the evening bell tolls for the dead!"

"You make me quite sad," said little Gerda. "I cannot help thinking of the dead maidens. Oh! is little Kay really dead? The Roses have been in the earth, and they say no."

"Ding, dong!" sounded the Hyacinth bells. "We do not toll for little Kay; we do not know him. That is our way of singing, the only one we have."

And Gerda went to the Ranunculuses, that looked forth from among the shining green leaves.

"You are a little bright sun!" said Gerda. "Tell me if you know where I can find my playfellow."

And the Ranunculus shone brightly, and looked again at Gerda. What song could the Ranunculus sing? It was one that said nothing about Kay either.

"In a small court the bright sun was shining in the first days of spring. The beams glided down the white walls of a neighbor's house, and close by the fresh yellow flowers were growing, shining like gold in the warm sunrays. An old Grandmother was sitting in the air; her Granddaughter, the poor and lovely servant just come for a short visit. She knows her Grandmother. There was gold, pure virgin gold, in that blessed kiss. There, that is my little story," said the Ranunculus.

"My poor old Grandmother!" sighed Gerda. "Yes, she is longing for me, no doubt; she is sorrowing for me, as she did for little Kay. But I will soon come home, and then I will bring Kay with me. It is of no use asking the Flowers; they only know their own old rhymes, and can tell me nothing." And she tucked up her frock, to enable her to run quicker; but the Narcissus gave her a knock on the leg, just as she was going to jump over it. So she stood still, looked at the long yellow flower, and asked, "You perhaps know something?" and she bent down to the Narcissus. And what did it say?

"I can see myself—I can see myself! Oh, how odorous I am! Up in the little garret there stands half-dressed a little Dancer. She stands now on one leg, now on both; she despises the whole world; yet she lives only in imagination. She pours water out of the teapot over a piece of stuff which she holds in her hand; it is the bodice: cleanliness is a fine thing. The white dress is hanging on the hook; it was washed in the teapot, and dried on the roof. She puts it on, ties a saffron-colored kerchief round her neck, and then the gown looks whiter. I can see myself—I can see myself!"

"That's nothing to me," said little Gerda. "That does not concern me." And then off she ran to the farther end of the garden.

The gate was locked, but she shook the rusted bolt till it was loosened, and the gate opened; and little Gerda ran off barefooted into the wide world. She looked round her thrice, but no one followed her. At last she could run no longer; she sat down on a large stone, and when she looked about her, she saw that the summer had passed; it was late in the autumn, but that one could not remark in the beautiful garden, where there was always sunshine, and where there were flowers the whole year round.

"Dear me, how long I have stayed!" said Gerda. "Autumn is come. I must not rest any longer." And she got up to go farther.

Oh, how tender and wearied her little feet were! All around, it looked so cold and raw; the long willow leaves were quite yellow, and the fog dripped from them like water; one leaf fell after the other: the sloes only stood full of fruit, which set one's teeth on edge. Oh, how dark and comfortless it was in the dreary world!

Fourth Story
THE PRINCE
AND PRINCESS

Gerda was obliged to rest herself again, when, exactly opposite to her, a large Raven came hopping over the white snow. He had long been looking at Gerda and shaking his head; and now he said, "Caw! caw!" Good day! good day! He could not say it better; but he felt a sympathy for the little girl, and asked her where she was going all alone. The word "alone" Gerda understood quite well, and felt how much was expressed by it; so she told the Raven her whole history, and asked if he had not seen Kay.

The Raven nodded very gravely, and said, "It may be—it may be!"

"What, do you really think so?" cried the little girl; and she nearly squeezed the Raven to death, so much did she kiss him.

"Gently, gently," said the Raven. "I think I know; I think that it may be little Kay. But now he has forgotten you for the Princess."

"Does he live with a Princess?" asked Gerda.

"Yes—listen," said the Raven; "but it will be difficult for me to speak your language. If you understand the raven language, I can tell you better."

"No, I have not learned it," said Gerda; "but my Grandmother understands it, and she can speak gibberish too. I wish I had learned it."

"No matter," said the Raven; "I will tell you as well as I can; however, it will be bad enough." And then he told all he knew.

"In the kingdom where we now are there lives a Princess, who is extraordinarily clever; for she has read all the newspapers in the whole world, and has forgotten them again—so clever is she. She was lately, it is said, sitting on her throne—which is not very amusing, after all—when she began humming an old tune, and it was just 'Oh, why should I not be married?' 'That song is not without its meaning,' said she, and so then she was determined to marry; but she would have a husband who knew how to give an answer when he was spoken to—not one who looked only as if he were a great personage, for that is so tiresome. She then had all the ladies of the court drummed together; and when they heard her intention, all were well pleased, and said, 'We are very glad to hear it; it is the very thing we were thinking of.' You may believe every word, I say," said the Raven; "for I have a tame sweetheart that hops about in the palace quite free, and it was she who told me all this.

"The newspapers appeared forthwith with a border of hearts and the initials of the Princess; and therein you might read that every good-looking young man was at liberty to come to the palace and speak to the Princess; and he who spoke in such wise as showed he felt himself at home there, that one the Princess would choose for her husband.

"Yes—yes," said the Raven, "you may believe it; it is as true as I am sitting here. People came in crowds; there was a crush and a hurry, but no one was successful either on the first or second day. They could all talk well enough when they were out in the street; but as soon as they came inside the palace gates, and saw the guard richly dressed in silver, and the lackeys in gold on the staircase, and the large illuminated salons, then they were abashed; and when they stood before the throne on which the Princess was sitting, all they could do was to repeat the last word they had uttered, and to hear it again did not interest her very much. It was just as if the people within were under a charm, and had fallen into a trance till they came out again into the street; for then—oh, then—they could chatter enough. There was a whole row of them standing from the town gates to the palace. I was there myself to look," said the Raven. "They grew hungry and thirsty; but from the palace they got nothing whatever, not even a glass of water. Some of the cleverest, it is true, had taken bread and butter with them; but none shared it with his neighbor, for each thought, 'Let him look hungry, and then the Princess won't have him.'"

"But Kay—little Kay," said Gerda, "when did he come? Was he among the number?"

"Patience, patience; we are just come to him. It was on the third day, when a little personage, without horse or equipage, came marching right boldly up to the palace; his eyes shone like yours, he had beautiful long hair, but his clothes were very shabby."

"That was Kay," cried Gerda, with a voice of delight. "Oh, now I've found him!" and she clapped her hands for joy.

· 30 ·   "He had a little knapsack at his back," said the Raven.

"No, that was certainly his sledge," said Gerda; "for when he went away he took his sledge with him."

"That may be," said the Raven; "I did not examine him so minutely: but I know from my tame sweetheart, that when he came into the courtyard of the palace, and saw the bodyguard in silver, the lackeys on the staircase, he was not the least abashed; he nodded, and said to them, 'It must be very tiresome to stand on the stairs; for my part, I shall go in.' The salons were gleaming with lusters—privy councillors and excellencies were walking about barefooted, and wore gold keys; it was enough to make anyone feel uncomfortable. His boots creaked, too, so loudly; but still he was not at all afraid."

"That's Kay, for certain," said Gerda. "I know he had on new boots; I have heard them creaking in Grandmamma's room."

"Yes, they creaked," said the Raven. "And on he went boldly up to the Princess, who was sitting on a pearl as large as a spinning wheel. All the ladies of the court, with their attendants and attendants' attendants, and all the cavaliers, with their gentlemen and gentlemen's gentlemen, stood round; and the nearer they stood to the door, the prouder they looked. It was hardly possible to look at the gentlemen's gentleman, so very haughtily did he stand in the doorway."

"It must have been terrible," said little Gerda. "And did Kay get the princess!"

"Were I not a Raven, I should have taken the Princess myself, although I am promised. It is said he spoke as well as I speak when I talk raven language; this I learned from my tame sweetheart. He was bold and nicely behaved; he had not come to woo the Princess, but only to hear her wisdom. She pleased him, and he pleased her."

"Yes, yes; for certain that was Kay," said Gerda. "He was so clever; he could reckon fractions in his head. Oh, won't you take me to the palace?"

"That is very easily said," answered the Raven. "But how are we to manage it? I'll speak to my tame sweetheart about it; she must advise us; for so much I must tell you, such a little girl as you are will never get permission to enter."

"Oh, yes, I shall," said Gerda; "when Kay hears that I am here, he will come out directly to fetch me."

"Wait for me here on these steps," said the Raven. He moved his head backward and forward, and flew away.

The evening was closing in when the Raven returned. "Caw, caw!" said he. "She sends you her compliments; and here is a roll for you. She took it out of the kitchen, where there is bread enough. You are hungry, no doubt. It is not possible for you to enter the palace, for you are barefooted; the guards in silver and the lackeys in gold would not allow it; but do not cry, you shall come in still. My sweetheart knows a little back stair that leads to the bedchamber, and she knows where she can get the key of it."

And they went into the garden in the large avenue, where one leaf was falling after the other; and when the lights in the palace had all gradually disappeared, the Raven led little Gerda to the back door, which stood half open.

Oh, how Gerda's heart beat with anxiety and longing! It was just as if she had been about to do something wrong; and yet she only wanted to know if little Kay was there. Yes, he must be there. She called to mind his intelligent eyes and his long hair so vividly, she could quite see him as he used to laugh when they were sitting under the roses at home. "He will, no doubt, be glad to see you—to hear what a long way you have come for his sake; to know how unhappy all at home were when he did not come back."

Oh, what a fright and a joy it was!

They were now on the stairs. A single lamp was burning there; and on the floor stood the tame Raven, turning her head on every side and looking at Gerda, who bowed as her grandmother had taught her to do.

"My intended has told me so much good of you, my dear young lady," said the tame Raven. "Your tale is very affecting. If you will take the lamp, I will go before. We will go straight on, for we shall meet no one."

"I think there is somebody just behind us," said Gerda; and something rushed past: it was like shadowy figures on the wall; horses with flowing manes and thin legs, huntsmen, ladies and gentlemen on horseback.

"They are only dreams," said the Raven. "They come to fetch the thoughts of the high personages to the chase: 'tis well, for now you can observe them in bed all the better. But let me find, when you enjoy honor and distinction, that you possess a grateful heart."

"Tut! that's not worth talking about," said the Raven of the woods.

They now entered the first salon, which was of rose-colored satin, with artificial flowers on the wall. Here the dreams were rushing past, but they hastened by so quickly, that Gerda could not see the high personages. One hall was more magnificent than the other; one might indeed well be abashed; and at last they came into the bedchamber. The ceiling of the room resembled a large palm tree with leaves of glass, of costly glass; and in the middle, from a thick golden stem, hung two beds, each of which resembled a lily. One was white, and in this lay the Princess: the other was red, and it was here that Gerda was to look for little Kay. She bent back one of the red leaves, and saw a brown neck. Oh! that was Kay! She called him quite loud by name, held the lamp toward him—the dreams rushed back again into the chamber—he awoke, turned his head, and—it was not little Kay!

The Prince was only like him about the neck; but he was young and handsome. And out of the white lily leaves the Princess peeped too, and asked what was the matter. Then little Gerda cried, and told her her whole history, and all that the Ravens had done for her.

"Poor little thing!" said the Prince and the Princess. They praised the Ravens very much, and told them they were not at all angry with them, but they were not to do so again. However they should have a reward.

"Will you fly about here at liberty," asked the Princess; "or would you like to have a fixed appointment as court ravens, with all the broken bits from the kitchen?"

And both the Ravens nodded, and begged for a fixed appointment; for they thought of their old age, and said, "it was a good thing to have a provision for their old days."

And the Prince got up and let Gerda sleep in his bed, and more than this he could not do. She folded her little hands, and thought, "how good men and animals are!" and she then fell asleep and slept soundly. All the dreams flew in again, and they now looked like the angels; they drew a little sledge, in which little Kay sat and nodded his head; but the whole was only a dream, and therefore it all vanished as soon as she awoke.

The next day she was dressed from head to foot in silk and velvet. They offered to let her stay at the palace, and lead a happy life; but she begged to have a little carriage with a horse in front, and for a small pair of shoes; then, she said, she would again go forth in the wide world, and look for Kay.

Shoes and a muff were given her; she was, too, dressed very nicely; and when she was about to set off, a new carriage stopped before the door. It was of pure gold, and the arms of the Prince and Princess shone like a star upon it; the coachman, the footmen, and the outriders, for outriders were there too, all wore golden crowns. The Prince and the Princess assisted her into the carriage themselves, and wished her all success. The Raven of the woods, who was now married, accompanied her for the first three miles. He sat beside Gerda, for he could not bear riding backward; the other Raven stood in the doorway, and flapped her wings; she could not accompany Gerda, because she suffered from headache since she had had a fixed appointment and ate so much. The carriage was lined inside with sugar-plums, and in the seats were fruits and gingerbread.

"Farewell! farewell!" cried Prince and Princess; and Gerda wept, and the Raven wept. Thus passed the first miles; and then the Raven bade her farewell, and this was the most painful separation of all. He flew into a tree, and beat his black wings as long as he could see the carriage, that shone from afar like a sunbeam.

THE LITTLE ROBBER-MAIDEN

They drove through the dark wood; but the carriage shone like a torch, and it dazzled the eyes of the robbers, so that they could not bear to look at it.

"'Tis gold! 'tis gold!" cried they; and they rushed forward, seized the horses, knocked down the little postilion, the coachman, and the servants, and pulled little Gerda out of the carriage.

"How plump, how beautiful she is! She must have been fed on nut kernels," said the old female Robber, who had a long scrubby beard, and bushy eyebrows that hung down over her eyes: "she is as good as a fatted lamb! how nice she will be!" And then she drew out a knife, the blade of which shone so that it was quite dreadful to behold.

"Oh!" cried the woman at the same moment. She had been bitten in the ear by her own little daughter, who hung at her back; and who was so wild and unmanageable that it was quite amusing to see her. "You naughty child!" said the mother; and now she had not time to kill Gerda.

"She shall play with me," said the little Robber-child: "she shall give me her muff, and her pretty frock; she shall sleep in my bed!" And then she gave her mother another bite, so that she jumped, and ran round with the pain; and the robbers laughed, and said, "Look how she is dancing with the little one!"

"I will go into the carriage," said the little Robber-maiden; and she would have her will, for she was very spoiled, and very headstrong. She and

Gerda got in; and then away they drove over the stumps of felled trees, deeper and deeper into the woods. The little Robber-maiden was as tall as Gerda, but stronger, broader-shouldered, and of dark complexion; her eyes were quite black; they looked almost melancholy. She embraced little Gerda, and said, "They shall not kill you as long as I am not displeased with you. You are, doubtless, a princess?"

"No," said little Gerda; who then related all that had happened to her, and how much she cared about little Kay.

The little Robber-maiden looked at her with a serious air, nodded her head slightly, and said, "They shall not kill you, even if I am angry with you: then I will do it myself"; and she dried Gerda's eyes, and put both her hands in the handsome muff, which was so soft and warm.

At length the carriage stopped. They were in the midst of the courtyard of a robber's castle. It was full of cracks from top to bottom; and out of the openings magpies and rooks were flying; and the great bulldogs, each of which looked as if he could swallow a man, jumped up, but they did not bark, for that was forbidden.

In the midst of the large, old, smoking hall burnt a great fire on the stone floor. The smoke disappeared under the stones, and had to seek its own egress. In an immense caldron soup was boiling; and rabbits and hares were being roasted on a spit.

"You shall sleep with me tonight, with all my animals," said the little Robber-maiden. They had something to eat and drink; and then went into a corner, where straw and carpets were lying. Beside them, on laths and perches, sat nearly a hundred pigeons, all asleep, seemingly; but yet they moved a little when the Robber-maiden came. "They are all mine," said she; at the same time seizing one that was next her by the legs, and shaking it so that its wings fluttered. "Kiss it," cried the little girl, and flung the pigeon in Gerda's face. "Up there is the rabble of the wood," continued she, pointing to several laths which were fastened before a hole high up in the wall; "that's the rabble; they would all fly away immediately, if they were not well fastened in. And here is my dear old Bac''; and she laid hold of the horns of a reindeer, that had a bright copper ring round its neck, and was tethered to the spot. ''We are obliged to lock this fellow in too, or he would make his escape. Every evening I tickle his neck with my sharp knife: he is so frightened at it!'' and the little girl drew forth a long knife, from a crack in the wall, and let it glide over the reindeer's neck. The poor animal kicked; the girl laughed, and pulled Gerda into bed with her.

''Do you intend to keep your knife while you sleep?'' asked Gerda; looking at it rather fearfully.

''I always sleep with the knife,'' said the little Robber-maiden: ''there is no knowing what may happen. But tell me now, once more, all about little Kay; and why you have started off in the wide world alone.'' And Gerda related all, from the very beginning: the wood pigeons cooed above in their cage, and the others slept. The little Robber-maiden wound her arm round Gerda's neck, held the knife in the other hand, and snored so loud that everybody could hear her; but Gerda could not close her eyes, for she did not know whether she was to live or die. The robbers sat round the fire, sang and drank; and the old female Robber jumped about so, that it was quite dreadful for Gerda to see her.

Then the Wood pigeons said, ''Coo! coo! we have seen little Kay! A white hen carries his sledge; he himself sat in the carriage of the Snow Queen, who passed here, down just over the wood, as we lay in our nest. She blew upon us young ones; and all died except we two. Coo! coo!''

''What is that you say up there?'' cried little Gerda. ''Where did the Snow Queen go to? Do you know anything about it?''

''She is no doubt gone to Lapland; for there is always snow and ice there. Only ask the Reindeer, who is tethered there.''

''Ice and snow is there! There it is glorious and beautiful!'' said the Reindeer. ''One can spring about in the large shining valleys! The Snow Queen has her summertent there; but her fixed abode is high up toward the North Pole, on the Island called Spitzbergen.''

"Oh, Kay! poor little Kay!" sighed Gerda.

"Do you choose to be quiet?" said the Robber-maiden. "If you don't, I shall make you."

In the morning Gerda told her all that the Wood pigeons had said; and the little maiden looked very serious, but she nodded her head and said, "That's no matter, that's no matter. Do you know where Lapland lies?" asked she of the Reindeer.

"Who should know better than I?" said the animal; and his eyes rolled in his head. "I was born and bred there—there I leapt about on the fields of snow."

"Listen," said the Robber-maiden to Gerda. "You see that the men are gone; but my mother is still here, and will remain. However, toward morning she takes a draft out of the large flask, and then she sleeps a little: then I will do something for you." She now jumped out of bed, flew to her mother; with her arms round her neck, and pulling her by the beard, said, "Good morrow, my own sweet nanny goat of a mother." And her mother took hold of her nose, and pinched it till it was red and blue; but this was all done out of pure love.

When the mother had taken a sup at her flask, and was having a nap, the little Robber-maiden went to the Reindeer, and said, "I should very much like to give you still many a tickling with the sharp knife, for then you are so amusing; however, I will untether you and help you out, so that you may get back to Lapland. But you must make good use of your legs; and take this little girl for me to the palace of the Snow Queen, where her play-fellow is. You have heard, I suppose, all she said; for she spoke loud enough, and you were listening."

The Reindeer gave a bound for joy. The Robber-maiden lifted up little Gerda, and took the precaution to bind her fast on the Reindeer's back; she even gave her a small cushion to sit on. "Here are your worsted leggings, for it will be cold; but the muff I shall keep for myself, for it is so very pretty. But I do not wish you to be cold. Here is a pair of lined gloves of my

mother's: they just reach up to your elbow. On with them! Now you look about the hands just like my ugly old mother!''

And Gerda wept for joy.

''I can't bear to see you fretting,'' said the little Robber-maiden. ''This is just the time when you ought to look pleased. Here are two loaves and a ham for you, so that you won't starve.'' The bread and the meat were fastened to the Reindeer's back; the little maiden opened the door, called in all the dogs, and then with her knife cut the rope that fastened the animal, and said to him, ''Now, off with you; but take good care of the little girl!''

And Gerda stretched out her hands with the large wadded gloves toward the Robber-maiden, and said, ''Farewell!'' and the Reindeer flew on over bush and bramble through the great wood, over moor and heath, as fast as he could go.

''Ddsa! ddsa!'' was heard in the sky. It was just as if somebody was sneezing.

''These are my old northern lights,'' said the Reindeer; ''look how they gleam!'' And on he now sped still quicker—day and night on he went: the loaves were consumed, and the ham too; and now they were in Lapland.

Sixth Story

THE LAPLAND WOMAN AND THE FINLAND WOMAN

Suddenly they stopped before a little house, which looked very miserable; the roof reached to the ground; and the door was so low, that the family was obliged to creep upon their stomachs when they went in or out. Nobody was at home except an old Lapland woman, who was dressing fish by the light of an oil lamp. And the Reindeer told her the whole of Gerda's history, but first of all his own; for that seemed to him of much greater importance. Gerda was so chilled that she could not speak.

"Poor thing," said the Lapland woman, "you have far to run still. You have more than a hundred miles to go before you get to Finland; there the Snow Queen has her country house, and burns blue lights every evening. I will give you a few words from me, which I will write on a dried haberdine, for paper I have none. This you can take with you to the Finland woman, and she will be able to give you more information than I can."

When Gerda had warmed herself, and had eaten and drunk, the Lapland woman wrote a few words on a dried haberdine, begged Gerda to take care of them, put her on the Reindeer, bound her fast, and away sprang the animal. "Ddsa! ddsa!" was again heard in the air; the most charming blue lights burned the whole night in the sky, and at last they came to Finland. They knocked at the chimney of the Finland woman; for as to a door, she had none.

There was such a heat inside that the Finland woman herself went about almost naked. She was diminuitive and dirty. She immediately loosened little Gerda's clothes, pulled off her thick gloves and boots; for otherwise the heat would have been too great—and after laying a piece of ice on the Reindeer's head, read what was written on the fish skin. She read it three times; she then knew it by heart; so she put the fish into the cupboard—for it might very well be eaten, and she never threw anything away.

Then the Reindeer related his own story first, and afterward that of little Gerda; and the Finland woman winked her eyes, but said nothing.

"You are so clever," said the Reindeer, "you can, I know, twist all the winds of the world together in a knot. If the seaman loosens one knot, then he has a good wind; if a second, then it blows pretty stiffly; if he undoes the third and fourth, then it rages so that the forests are upturned. Will you give the little maiden a potion, that she may possess the strength of twelve men, and vanquish the Snow Queen?"

"The strength of twelve men!" said the Finland woman. "Much good that would be!" Then she went to a cupboard, and drew out a large skin rolled up. When she had unrolled it, strange characters were to be seen written thereon; and the Finland woman read at such a rate that the perspiration trickled down her forehead.

But the Reindeer begged so hard for little Gerda, and Gerda looked so imploringly with tearful eyes at the Finland woman, that she winked and drew the Reindeer aside into a corner, where they whispered together, while the animal got some fresh ice put on his head.

"'Tis true little Kay is at the Snow Queen's, and finds everything there quite to his taste; and he thinks it the very best place in the world: but the reason of that is, he has a splinter of glass in his eye and in his heart. These must be got out first; otherwise he will never go back to mankind, and the Snow Queen will retain her power over him."

"But can you give little Gerda nothing to take which will endue her with power over the whole?"

"I can give her no more power than what she has already. Don't you see how great it is? Don't you see how men and animals are forced to serve her; how well she gets through the world barefooted? She must not hear of her power from us: that power lies in her heart, because she is a sweet and innocent child! If she cannot get to the Snow Queen by herself, and rid little Kay of the glass, we cannot help her. Two miles hence the garden of the Snow Queen begins; thither you may carry the little girl. Set her down by the large bush with red berries, standing in the snow; don't stay talking, but hasten back as fast as possible." And now the Finland woman placed little Gerda on the Reindeer's back, and off he ran with all imaginable speed.

"Oh! I have not got my boots! I have not brought my gloves!" cried little Gerda. She remarked she was without them from the cutting frost: but the Reindeer dared not stand still; on he ran till he came to the great bush with the red berries, and there he set Gerda down, kissed her mouth,

while large bright tears flowed from the animal's eyes, and then back he went as fast as possible. There stood poor Gerda now, without shoes or gloves, in the very middle of dreadful icy Finland.

She ran on as fast as she could. There then came a whole regiment of snowflakes, but they did not fall from above, and they were quite bright and shining from the Aurora Borealis. The flakes ran along the ground, and the nearer they came the larger they grew. Gerda well remembered how large and strange the snowflakes appeared when she once saw them through a magnifying glass; but now they were large and terrific in another manner—they were all alive. They were the outposts of the Snow Queen. They had the most wondrous shapes; some looked like large ugly porcupines; others like snakes knotted together, with their heads sticking out; and others, again, like small fat bears, with the hair standing on end: all were of dazzling whiteness—all were living snowflakes.

Little Gerda repeated the Lord's Prayer. The cold was so intense that she could see her own breath, which came like smoke out of her mouth. It grew thicker and thicker, and took the form of little angels, that grew more and more when they touched the earth. All had helms on their heads, and lances and shields in their hands; they increased in numbers; and when Gerda had finished the Lord's Prayer, she was surrounded by a whole legion. They thrust at the horrid snowflakes with their spears, so that they flew into a thousand pieces; and little Gerda walked on bravely and in security. The angels patted her hands and feet; and then she felt the cold less, and went on quickly toward the palace of the Snow Queen.

But now we shall see how Kay fared. He never thought of Gerda, and least of all that she was standing before the palace.

Seventh Story
WHAT TOOK PLACE IN THE PALACE OF THE SNOW QUEEN, AND WHAT HAPPENED AFTERWARD

The walls of the palace were of driving snow, and the windows and doors of cutting winds. There were more than a hundred halls there, according as the snow was driven by the winds. The largest was many miles in extent; all were lighted up by the powerful Aurora Borealis, and all were so large, so empty, so icy cold, and so resplendent! Mirth never reigned there; there was never even a little bear ball, with the storm for music, while the polar bears went on their hind legs and showed off their steps. Never a little tea party of white young lady foxes; vast, cold, and empty were the halls of the Snow Queen. The northern lights shone with such precision that one could tell exactly when they were at their highest or lowest degree of brightness.

In the middle of the empty, endless hall of snow, was a frozen lake; it was cracked in a thousand pieces, but each piece was so like the other, that it seemed the work of a cunning artificer. In the middle of this lake sat the Snow Queen when she was at home; and then she said she was sitting in the Mirror of Understanding, and that this was the only one and the best thing in the world.

Little Kay was quite blue, yes, nearly black with cold; but he did not observe it, for she had kissed away all feeling of cold from his body, and his heart was a lump of ice. He was dragging along some pointed flat pieces of ice, which he laid together in all possible ways, for he wanted to make something with them; just as we have little flat pieces of wood to make geometrical figures with, called the Chinese Puzzle. Kay made all sorts of figures, the most complicated, for it was an ice puzzle for the understanding. In his eyes the figures were extraordinarily beautiful, and of the utmost importance; for the bit of glass which was in his eye caused this. He found whole figures which represented a written word; but he never could manage to represent just the word he wanted—that word was "eternity"; and the Snow Queen had said, "If you can discover that figure, you shall be your own master, and I will make you a present of the whole world and a pair of new skates." But he could not find it out.

"I am going now to the warm lands," said the Snow Queen. "I must have a look down into the black caldrons." It was the volcanoes Vesuvius and Etna that she meant. "I will just give them a coating of white, for that is as it ought to be; besides, it is good for the oranges and the grapes." And then away she flew, and Kay sat quite alone in the empty halls of ice that were miles long, and looked at the blocks of ice, and thought till his skull was almost cracked. There he sat quite benumbed and motionless; one would have imagined he was frozen to death.

Suddenly little Gerda stepped through the great portal into the palace. The gate was formed of cutting winds; but Gerda repeated her evening prayer, and the winds were laid as though they slept; and the little maiden entered the vast, empty, cold halls. There she beheld Kay: she recognized

him, flew to embrace him, and cried out, her arms firmly holding him the while, "Kay, sweet little Kay! Have I then found you at last?"

But he sat quite still, benumbed and cold. Then little Gerda shed burning tears; and they fell on his bosom, they penetrated to his heart, they thawed the lumps of ice, and consumed the splinters of the looking-glass: he looked at her, and she sang the hymn:

> The rose in the valley is blooming so sweet,
> And angels descend there the children to greet.

Hereupon Kay burst into tears; he wept so much that the splinter rolled out of his eye, and he recognized her, and shouted, "Gerda, sweet little Gerda! where have you been so long? And where have I been?" He looked round him. "How cold it is here!" said he; "how empty and cold!" And he held fast to Gerda, who laughed and wept for joy. It was so beautiful, that even the blocks of ice danced about for joy; and when they were tired and laid themselves down, they formed exactly the letters which the Snow Queen had told him to find out; so now he was his own master, and he would have the whole world and a pair of new skates into the bargain.

Gerda kissed his cheeks, and they grew quite blooming; she kissed his eyes, and they shone like her own; she kissed his hands and feet, and he was again well and merry. The Snow Queen might come back as soon as she liked; there stood his discharge written in resplendent masses of ice.

They took each other by the hand, and wandered forth out of the large hall; they talked of their old grandmother, and of the roses upon the roof; and wherever they went, the winds ceased raging, and the sun burst forth. And when they reached the bush with the red berries, they found the Reindeer waiting for them. He had brought another, a young one, with him, whose udder was filled with milk, which he gave to the little ones, and kissed their lips. They then carried Kay and Gerda—first to the Finland woman, where they warmed themselves in the warm room, and learned what they were to do on their journey home; and then they went to the Lapland woman, who made some new clothes for them and repaired their sledges.

The Reindeer and the young hind leaped along beside them, and accompanied them to the boundary of the country. Here the first vegetation peeped forth; here Kay and Gerda took leave of the Lapland woman. "Farewell! farewell!" said they all. And the first green buds appeared, the first little birds began to chirrup; and out of the wood came, riding on a magnificent horse, which Gerda knew (it was one of the leaders in the golden carriage), a young damsel with a bright red cap on her head, and armed with pistols. It was the little Robber-maiden, who, tired of being at home, had determined to make a journey to the north; and afterward in another direction, if that did not please her. She recognized Gerda immediately, and Gerda knew her too. It was a joyful meeting.

"You are a fine fellow for tramping about," said she to little Kay; "I should like to know, faith, if you deserve that one should run from one end of the world to the other for your sake?"

But Gerda patted her cheeks, and inquired for the Prince and Princess.

"They are gone abroad," said the other.

"But the Raven?" asked little Gerda.

"Oh! the Raven is dead," answered she. "His tame sweetheart is a widow, and wears a bit of black worsted round her leg; she laments most piteously, but it's all mere talk and stuff! Now tell me what you've been doing, and how you managed to catch him."

And Gerda and Kay both told her their story.

And "Schnipp-schnapp-schnurre-basselurre" said the Robber-maiden; and she took the hands of each, and promised that if she should some day pass through the town where they lived, she would come and visit them; and then away she rode. Kay and Gerda took each other's hand: it was lovely spring weather, with abundance of flowers and of verdure. The church bells rang, and the children recognized the high towers, and the large town; it was that in which they dwelt. They entered, and hastened up

to their Grandmother's room, where everything was standing as formerly. The clock said "tick! tack!" and the finger moved round; but as they entered, they remarked that they were now grown up. The roses on the leads hung blooming in at the open window; there stood the little children's chairs, and Kay and Gerda sat down on them, holding each other by the hand: they both had forgotten the cold empty splendor of the Snow Queen, as though it had been a dream. The Grandmother sat in the bright sunshine, and read aloud from the Bible: "Unless ye become as little children, ye cannot enter the kingdom of heaven."

And Kay and Gerda looked in each other's eyes, and all at once they understood the old hymn:

The rose in the valley is blooming so sweet,
And angels descend there the children to greet.

There sat the two grown-up persons; grown-up, and yet children; children at least in heart: and it was summertime; summer, glorious summer!

Afterword

Not all children grow up. There are those who in maturity can vividly recall every little hurt, every brief joy, every small victory encountered in infancy, but this rare ability is more the work of an extraordinary memory than of an absence of emotional growth. Others, however, experience such intense childhoods that, although they grow older in years, the continue to feel, think, and react exactly as they did when little. For each of these, the child is not father to the man ; the child never really becomes the man. Often these people write or illustrate books for boys and girls.

Just such a person was Hans Christian Andersen (1805–1875). "I was a singularly dreamy child," the Danish poet recalled in his autobiography, "and so constantly went about with my eyes shut, as at last to give the impression of having weak sight, although the sense of sight was especially cultivated by me." So strange was this poor cobbler's son that many thought he must be a fool like his weak-minded grandfather. Tall, awkward, and ugly, the boy was lonely; he preferred to play with the puppet theater his father made for him rather than with the other children of Odense. His mother was so troubled by his odd behavior that she consulted a witch, who advised that he be dunked in an enchanted spring to shake him back to his senses. Little changed even when he was sent to school. "Often I sat dreaming and gazing on the variegated wall," he recollected; and for his absentmindedness the child was reprimanded by the master of the charity school he attended. "I told the boys curious stories in which I was always the chief person, but was sometimes rallied for that. The street lads had also heard from their parents of my peculiar turn of mind.... I was therefore one day pursued by a wild crowd of them, who shouted after me derisively, 'There goes the play-writer!' I hid myself at home in a corner, cried, and prayed to God."

But this grotesque child also had a marvelous singing voice, and his neighbors encouraged him to go to Copenhagen to follow a career in the theater. His mother did not at first approve; she thought it better that her son learn the tailor's trade, and changed her mind only after she had again consulted a witch, who through coffee grounds and cards predicted: "Your son will become a great man and in honor of him Odense will one day be illuminated." So at age fourteen, with a little money in his pocket, Hans Christian Andersen departed on foot to the Danish capital to seek his fortune. His singing career ended when his voice changed, however; and only after many years of struggle (coupled with some good luck) did the poor shoemaker's son become one of Denmark's most famous writers.

Through his fairy tales, Andersen became the children's friend. "In the streets and from the windows," he wrote of his life in Copenhagen, "there often nodded after me a friendly child's face. I met one day a well-dressed lady walking with her children; the smallest boy broke away, ran over to me, and seized me by the hand. The mother called to him and said, 'How dare you accost a strange gentleman!' but the little fellow replied, 'It was no stranger, it was Andersen; all the boys know him.'" Even in middle age, the poet retained the semblance of still being a boy himslef. "He looks like a large child, a sort of half angel," the English poet William Allingham noted in his diary after a glimpse of the Danish writer at a party in London. "There were many people of rank present, yet no one in the room looked more *distingué* than Andersen, the shoemaker's son." Even after he was internationally lauded for his writings, Andersen remained emotionally much a child. He might weep at the smallest provocation, on reading a bad review of one of his books or on not receiving the largest slice of cake at dinner. But certainly it was just this failure to fully put aside childish things which helped distinguish Andersen's work from that of his contemporaries. "I had written my narrative down upon paper exactly in the language, and with the expressions in which I had myself related them, by word of mouth, to the little ones," he once described his working method, "and I had arrived at the conviction that people of different ages were equally amused with them. The children made themselves merry for the most part over what might be called the actors; older people, on the contrary, were interested in the deeper meaning." That he succeeded in his fairy tales to entertain both children and their elders was, as he himself admitted, "a difficult task for those who will write children's stories."

Like Hans Christian Andersen, Kate Greenaway (1846–1901) was a dreamy, lonely child. "I was never told I was tiresome when I was young," she later disclosed, "but I was constantly told I was *odd*." This imaginative little girl used to invent "delightful places just close and unexpected." Recalling her London childhood, she wrote: "My bedroom windows used to look out over red roofs and chimney pots, and I made steps up into a lovely garden up there with nasturtiums growing and brilliant flowers so near to the sky. There were some old houses joined ours at the sides, and I made a secret door into long lines of old rooms, all so delightful, leading into an old garden. I imagined it so often that I knew its look so well, it got to be very real." So vivid was this private world, her "Somewhere Town," that when she grew up, the "mixed child and woman" (as John Ruskin called her) recreated this blissful country in *Under the Window, Marygold Garden*, and the other pretty picture books which she illustrated and sometimes wrote as well. "I had such a very happy time when I was a child," the artist once confided to a friend. "I suppose my imaginary life made me one long joy—filled everything with a strange most wonder and beauty. Living in that childish wonder is a most beautiful feeling—I can so well remember it. There was always something more—behind and beyond everything—to me; the golden spectacles were very very big." Her unusual childlike sympathies, expressed through delicately drawn and colored pictures of boys and girls, dressed in her unique interpretation of archaic costume, made her little works, like Andersen's efforts, appealing equally to adults and children of the Victorian age.

Ironically, although both earned their greatest reputations from their books for the young, neither Hans Christian Andersen nor Kate Greenaway had any children of their own. The ugly boy grew into an ugly man. "I was almost painfully struck, at the first moment, by the grotesque ugliness of his face and hands, and by his enormously long and swinging arms," Edmund Gosse described Andersen in *Two Visits to Denmark*; "but this impression passed away as soon as he began to speak. His eyes, although they were small, had great sweatness and vivacity of expression, while gentleness and ingenuousness breathed from everything he said." The plain girl grew into a plain woman. "I was given quite the wrong sort of body to live in, I am sure," Greenaway once admitted. "I ought to have been taller, slimmer, and at any rate passably good-looking, so that my soul might have taken flights, my fancy might have expanded." But what she lacked in physical grace the artist more than made up for in brisk talk, merry laughter, and a simple, natural character. Neither Andersen nor Greenaway married; and although each suffered from childish crushes (he on Jenny Lind, she on John Ruskin), there is no evidence that either had an active sexual life. Andersen, however, had no regrets. He proudly began his autobiography, "My life is a lovely story, happy and full of incident." Greenaway too confessed to having a generally happy view of the world. "People laugh at me," she told a friend, "I am so delighted and pleased with things, and say I see with rose-coloured spectacles. What do you think—is it not a beautiful world?"

Even when a woman, Kate Greenaway was drawn to fairytales and in particular to those by Hans Christian Andersen. She likely knew them from her childhood (the earliest English translations began appearing in 1846, the year of her birth); but it was not until the last year of her life that she attempted illustrating any of the famous stories. Although from 1878 with the publication of *Under the Window* Greenaway became England's perhaps most popular children's-book artist, she devoted more of her time during the 1890s to watercolors for exhibition and less to books for boys and girls; the only ones issued during the last decade of the nineteenth century were her almanacs and calendars. Under John Ruskin's guidance, she had harbored hopes of becoming a distinguished British painter, and consequently she allowed her reputation as an illustrator to fade. Perhaps with some relief, she confessed to Ruskin that she felt the fashion for her books had passed by then: "I say fashion, for that is the right word, that is all I am to a great many people." But when her master died in 1900, she bravely tried to revive her career as a picture book artist. Although suffering severe pain from breast cancer, she ambitiously planned many new and varied book projects. Pencil studies and some finished watercolors were made for many of these: a new volume of *Nursery Rhymes; Baby's Debut; A Book of Girls;* a collection of her own "sonnets"; and her interpretations of Blake's *Songs of Innocence*, and Andersen's *What the Moon Saw* and *The Snow Queen*. Unfortunately, publishers were noncommittal, and none of these charming schemes ever reached fruition. Instead, she had to accept a commission to illustrate an unremarkable work by another, *The April Baby's Book of Tunes* by Countess von Arnim, with unhappy results. This children's book, with its unremarkable pictures, was her last published work; she died in November 1901.

Of her aborted projects, one that was particularly suited to Kate Greenaway's sensibilities was *The Snow Queen*. This exquisite story, more a novella than a tale, may be Andersen's masterpiece. Begun in 1844 while he was a guest of Lieutenant Serre and his gracious wife at their country estate in Maxen near Dresden, Germany, and completed on his return to Copenhagen, the story of devoted Gerda's search for little Kay was partially autobiographical. In describing the apartments where the two children lived, Andersen recalled his own poor home when a boy in Odense:

> Our little room, which was almost filled with the shoemaker's bench, the bed, and my crib, was the abode of my childhood; the walls, however, were covered with pictures, and over the work-bench was a cupboard containing books and songs; the little kitchen was full of shining plates and metal pans, and by means of a ladder it was possible to go out on the roof, where in the gutters between it and the neighbor's house, there stood a great chest filled with soil, my mother's sole garden, and where she grew her vegetables. In my story of the "Snow Queen" that garden still blooms.

The Snow Queen's abduction of the little boy was inspired by the day Andersen's father died, when a cricket chirped the whole night through.

> "He is dead," said my mother, addressing it; "thou needest not call him. The ice maiden has fetched him."

> I understood what she meant. I recollected that, in the winter before, when our window-panes were frozen, my father pointed to them and showed us a figure like that of a maiden with outstretched arms. "She is come to fetch me," said he, in jest. And now, when he lay dead on the bed, my mother remembered this, and it occupied my thoughts also.

Thus Gerda's guest is to return her beloved Kay from the land of the Dead; to

Andersen, apparently, Hell was not fire but ice. Subtly the poet altered his father's legend in the fairy tale: The demon lover has been transformed into a barren spirit in search of a little boy of her own.

Happily, the drawings that Kate Greenaway made for the proposed book, twelve pencil studies, all survive. Her scheme for *The Snow Queen* was a departure from her usual work. Most of Greenaway's picture books were collections of verse and, except for some early toy books, rarely fairy tales; the few stories that she did illustrate were often either mundane (such as Beatrice F. Cresswell's *The Royal Progress of King Pepito*) or ill suited to her style (such as Bret Harte's *The Queen of Pirate Island*). Perhaps she resisted lengthy narratives because she had some difficulty sustaining characters throughout an entire story. But she had no such worry with *The Snow Queen*: The only ones whom she had to carry through the story were Gerda and Kay, and she had no trouble in drawing children.

As for the subjects of her drawings, many follow the classic illustrations by Vilhelm Pedersen, Andersen's Danish illustrator, for the first authorized collection of the fairy tales; these designs were perhaps the most frequently reprinted of Andersen illustrations during the nineteenth century. However, Greenaway's graceful drawings avoided the woodenness that mars the generally uninspired Pedersen decorations. Also, *The Snow Queen* allowed the English artist's fancy to roam more freely than it had in the majority of her earlier projects. Few of her designs are lovelier than her studies of the Snow Queen herself, and none more alarming than her grotesque (and uncharacteristic) depiction of the demon with the enchanted mirror.

The twelve drawings are mere sketches, unfinished studies in delicate outline. Nevertheless, they clearly define what Kate Greenaway had intended for the published work: They fully illustrate the text, and it is unlikely that the artist hoped to add any further designs to this dozen. Even in this unfinished state, this suite of drawings for *The Snow Queen* offers an unusually sensitive interpretation of the Andersen fairy tale by one of the greatest of English children's book artists.

Michael Patrick Hearn